TO:

FROM:

Because this
book found YOU.

YOU WILL be FOUND

BENJ PASEK · JUSTIN PAUL

ILLUSTRATED BY

SARAH J. COLEMAN

LITTLE, BROWN AND COMPANY

NEW YORK   BOSTON

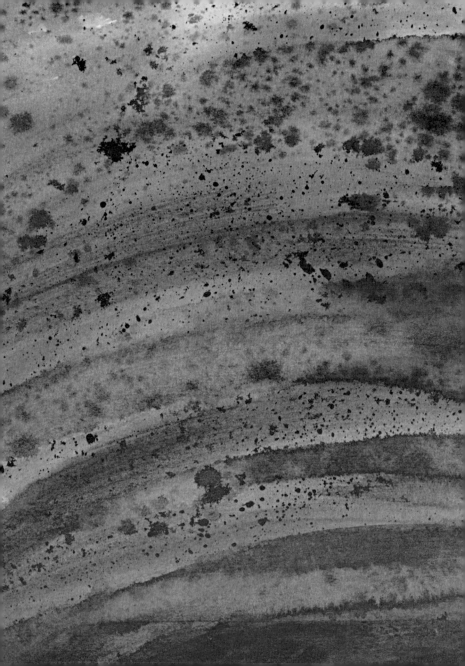

A MESSAGE from BENJ and JUSTIN

When we wrote "You Will Be Found" for our Broadway musical *Dear Evan Hansen*, it was to solve a problem: We needed a moment at the end of the first act for the main character, Evan, to decide to stand up—to literally pick himself up off the ground—and move forward. In the scene, Evan is in front of a crowd recalling a dark moment he experienced, and the pain and loneliness he felt drives him to reimagine his story, to consider how everything might have been different if he'd had someone he could reach out to. We wanted music and lyrics that felt propulsive and optimistic yet emotionally vulnerable. The song became one in which Evan opens himself up to the possibility of connecting with someone and feeling understood. The song also sets in motion a moment that goes viral in the world of the show.

And then something fascinating happened. Beyond the context of the stage musical, the song did what Evan hoped to do with his story: It connected. And it went viral. We heard from so many people around the world who found comfort in being reminded that they are not alone. The message at the core of the song resonated, and reverberated—in our darkest moments and loneliest times, if we are willing to be vulnerable and reach out, we can find a support system and community waiting to help us.

The response we got—and witnessed online—is what led to the book you're holding. We were inspired to publish it by the fans of the show, and particularly of the song, who took ownership of the message and made these lyrics their own. Who recorded covers, posted videos online, started social media groups; a community connecting people who wanted to be found with those who were there to find them. We wrote the song for a specific character on a particular journey, and now it's taken on a life of its own. So we've recreated it in this tangible form for anyone who needs to hear, or share, its message.

This book is for anyone on the edge of a new chapter in life—whether it's graduating from school, moving across the country, starting a new job, working through a tough time, or simply taking a chance on the unknown. It is a reminder that when you don't know where your past will lead you next, when your future is uncertain, or when you want to be seen or understood, you can reach out, call out, and discover that you are anything but alone. Because there is always someone there. Maybe it's someone sitting next to you, maybe it's somebody you haven't even met yet, or maybe it's the person who gave you this book. But as you read these words, remember that we are all connected and…you will be found.

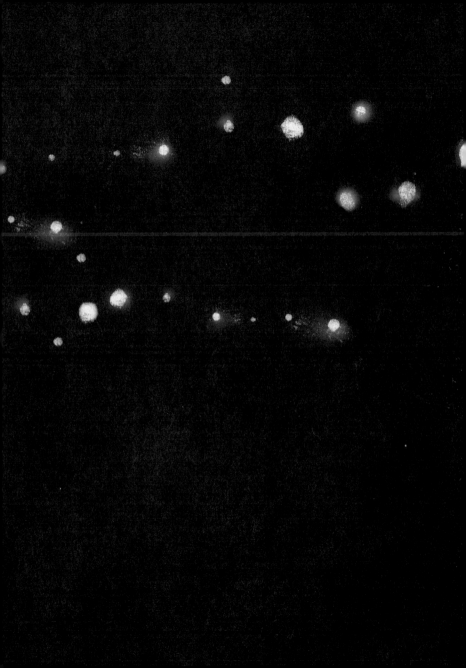

HAVE YOU
EVER
FELT
LIKE

NOBODY
WAS
THERE?

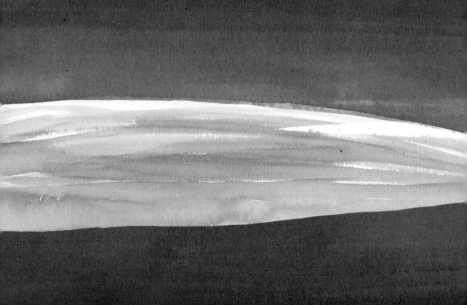

Have you ever felt FORGOTTEN

in the middle
of NOWHERE?

Have you
ever felt like
you could

disappear?

and
no one
would
hear?

Well,

LET THAT
LONELY FEELING
wash away

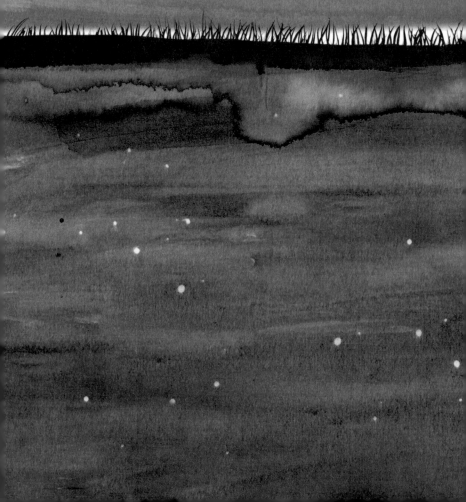

MAYBE THERE'S A REASON
TO BELIEVE

you'll be
OKAY

'CAUSE
WHEN
YOU
DON'T
FEEL
STRONG
ENOUGH
TO
STAND
YOU
CAN

REACH

REACH OUT your HAND

And someone will come running

to
take
you
home

EVEN WHEN THE DARK. COMES CRASHING THROUGH

When you
need a
friend

TO CARRY YOU

AND
WHEN
YOU'RE

BROKEN

ON
THE
GROUND

You

WILL *be* FOUND

so let the
SUN
come streaming in
'Cause you'll reach up
and you'll RISE AGAIN

LIFT YOUR HEAD

and

look

around

YOU WILL be FOUND

There's a place
where we don't
have to feel
UNKNOWN
and
every time
that you
call out

you're a
little
less
ALONE

If you only
only

say
the
word

FROM ACROSS
THE SILENCE
YOUR VOICE
IS HEARD

someone will come running to take you home SOMEONE WILL COME

take you home SOMEONE WILL CO

KE YOU HOME THE someone wil

ne SOMEONE WORLD to take you

NNING to NEEDS WILL COME RU

to take you to HEAR TAKE YOU

KE YOU HOME THIS home SOME

meone will come runn

LL COME Share it RUNNING

g to take you love you hom
with people

SOMEONE WILL COME RUN

WILL COME RUNN

come running to tak

nning to take you h

IT'S SO EASY TO feel ALONE

EVEN WHEN THE DARK COMES CRASHING THROUGH

WHEN YOU NEED A FRIEND TO CARRY YOU

WHEN YOU'RE BROKEN ON THE GROUND

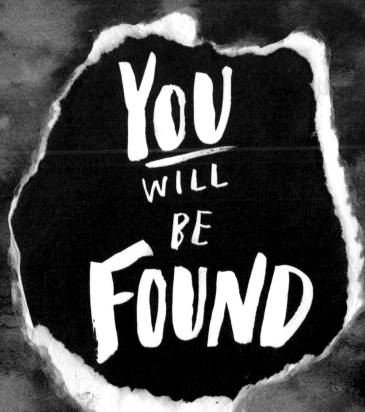

Out of the shadows
the morning is
breaking

and all is
new,
all is new

IT'S FILLING UP
THE
EMPTY
AND SUDDENLY
YOU SEE

THAT ALL IS NEW,
ALL
IS
NEW

YOU

ARE
NOT
ALONE

you are not alone
YOU ARE NOT
You are not alone x
YOU
YOU ARE NOT ALONE
You are not ALONE

You are not
alone

You are
not
alone

you are
not alone

NOT ALONE

YOU ARE
NOT
ALONE

you are
not
alone

YOU
You are not alone
You are not alone
You are not alone
YOU ARE NOT ALONE
You are not alone

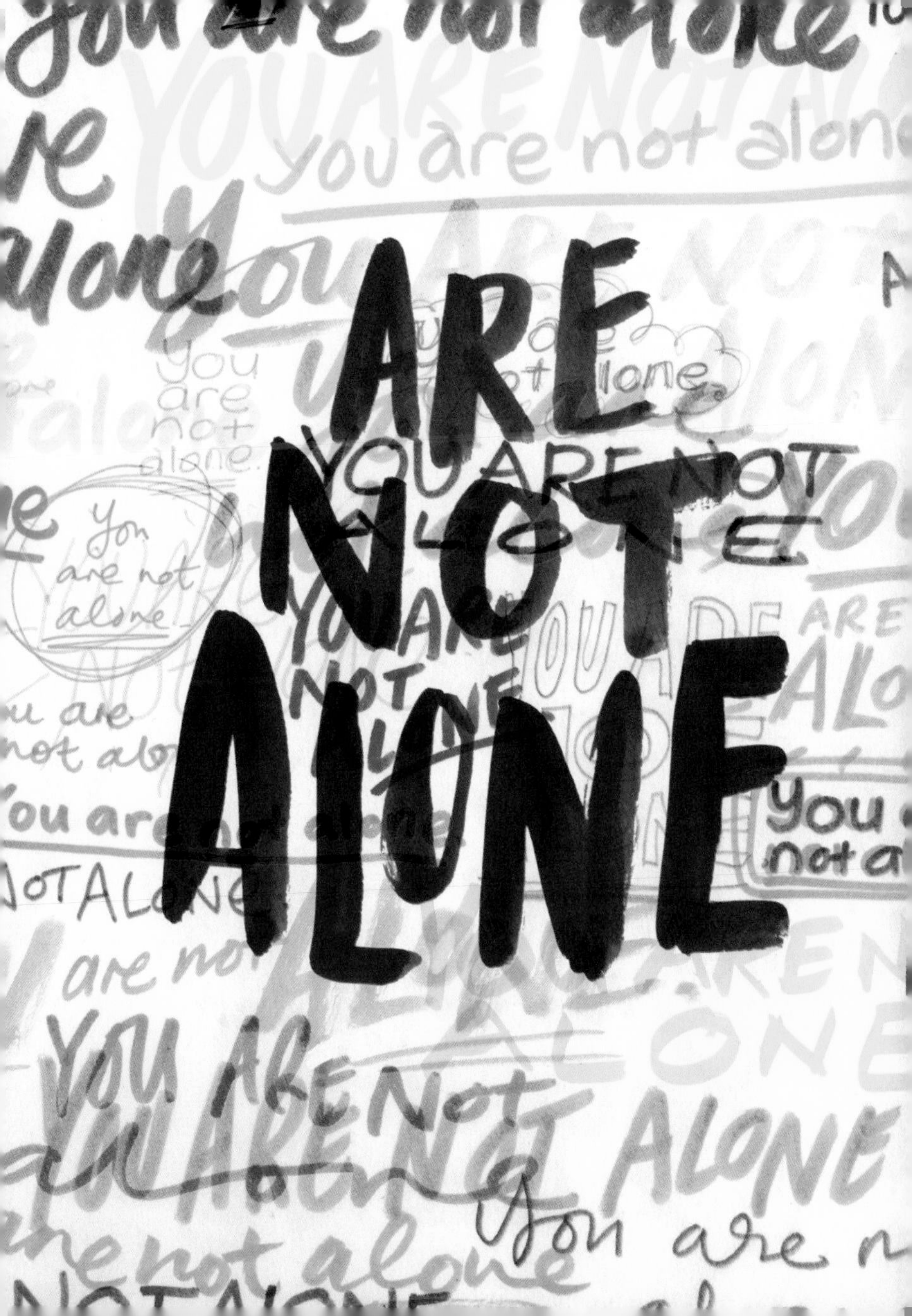

EVEN WHEN THE DARK COMES CRASHING THROUGH

WHEN YOU NEED SOMEONE TO CARRY YOU

WHEN YOU'RE BROKEN ON THE GROUND

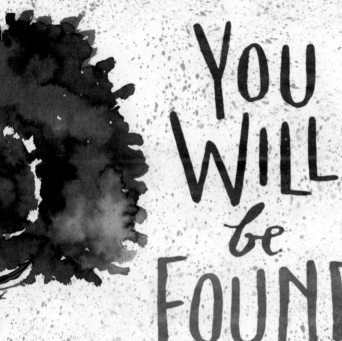

ACKNOWLEDGMENTS

First, we would like to thank the fans of the musical. Your enthusiasm for *Dear Evan Hansen* and this song has meant so much to us, and this book exists because of you.

Thanks to Steven Levenson, our brilliant collaborator and friend, as well as Stacey Mindich, Michael Greif, and the entire *Dear Evan Hansen* family. Additional thanks to Jordan Carroll, Drew Cohen, Abby Faber, Freddie Gershon, Cait Hoyt, Joe Machota, Jeff Marx, Asher Paul, Ben Platt, Marc Platt, Adam Siegel, Aly Solot, and Jack Viertel.

To the team at Little, Brown Books for Young Readers, including but not limited to David Caplan, Jen Graham, Karina Granda, Sasha Illingworth, and Farrin Jacobs, as well as Sarah J. Coleman, thank you for helping to turn our lyrics into something we can all hold on to.

A NOTE from MICHAEL GREIF

When I heard "You Will Be Found" for the first time, I knew it was the right fit for that moment in the show, when the emotions are so heightened and Evan feels so very lost. But none of us anticipated that it would resonate with people in such a significant way. For anyone listening to "You Will Be Found" on the cast recording, without seeing the show, it's a beautiful song about fitting in and not feeling alone; it takes on a much more complex meaning when you're watching it in the theater, in the context of what's happening in the show, which is one of the most brilliant things about it. As *Dear Evan Hansen* expands beyond Broadway to other cities and other countries, it's amazing to know that Benj and Justin's beautiful music and lyrics will continue to make people feel a little less alone in this world.

Michael Greif *is the director of seven Broadway shows, including the original productions of* Dear Evan Hansen, Next to Normal, *and* Rent.

If you or a loved one are in need of help, please know: You are not alone.

The following organizations are good resources:

Born This Way Foundation: bornthisway.foundation

Child Mind Institute: childmind.org

Crisis Text Line: crisistextline.org

The illustrations for this book were done in ink, pencil, charcoal, monoprinting, felt pens, and bleach on 300 gsm cartridge paper. This book was edited by Farrin Jacobs and designed by Sasha Illingworth. The production was supervised by Virginia Lawther, and the production editor was Jen Graham. The text was set in Adobe Garamond Pro, and the display type was hand-lettered by Sarah J. Coleman.